Mirage t[...]

Ratish Kanta Sen

Published by Walnut Publication

#722, Esplanade One, Rasulgarh

Bhubaneswar - 751010, India

www.walnutpublication.com

ISBN: 9788194272281

First Published in October 2019

Contents

Chapter-1 1

Chapter-2 4

Chapter-3 8

Chapter-4 11

Chapter-5 14

Chapter-6 19

Chapter-7 22

Chapter-8 25

Chapter-9 28

Chapter-10 31

Chapter-11 36

Chapter-12 38

Chapter-13 44

Chapter-14 47

Chapter-15 50

Chapter-16 53

Chapter-17 56

Chapter-18 59

Chapter-19 62

Chapter-20 67

Chapter-21 69

Chapter-22 72

Chapter-23 74

Chapter-24 77

Chapter-25 81

Chapter-26 85

Chapter-27 89

Chapter-28 92

Chapter-29 94

Chapter-30 102

Chapter-1

The sun waving its rays over the cool stream, beside the field of wheat, the breeze swinging to its fullest amidst the green leaves of neem. The colourful village girls in yellow, red green, orange and many more under the mango grove giggling, dancing, sitting and pushing one another in the rope swing while singing. The mother nature showering her bliss; cuckoo coos to orchestra the song of the girls. Small kids collecting mango beneath the trees; Shina a girl of 13 years busy in sickling the weight laden wheat in the field, smiling sweet like the crescent in the sky.

 The field , mango groves,neem tree ,the jocund air is all about to describe our bliss of Punjab. A small village in the extreme west kissing the border of Pakistan, Fazilka, people rarely know about the existence of this small place. About 200 kms. South of Amritsar. The village is composed of tradition, rich culture, in fact a prosperous picture of the mini India of then. India was in her 2nd 5th year plan crawling hard to stand firmly. Besides rural folks, less literate,

Orthodox mentality and patriarchal influence in the society ruled profoundly.

All the girls enjoying all the possible way they could; except Shina, who was sent in this earth to perform every aspect's duty. To be friendly with happiness, amusement and pleasure, she never felt off herself. These are abstract dreams to be touched. Shina being an introvert girl, exclaimed her self to the call of other girls from the gleeful playground;… "my little life ground is my wheat and bazra field…..my lil life entertainment is to care for my parents, I have no time to waste, rather I'll enjoy seeing others happy".

Shina was the only girl child after three brothers in the family of Rajinder. Raghuveer, Rajveer and Ranjit Singh. They were loved with all tender and care of parents, taoji(uncle), taiji(aunt) and their sons loved them just like princes. The Singhs had a wealthy background since the British raj. In Punjab they had a legacy from their fore-father. Rajinder Singh, the father and Shalini Singh Shina's mother were very aristocratic and patriarchal in attitude. It's just after few years of Indian independence, the month of January on 15th when one of the suffering soul blinked on her carnal eyes beneath the almighty's blue. The entire bungalow was as cold as chilly January.

" this was our final consideration into our clan. Oh! And we are to bear a damsel".….. murmured Rajinder . " arre o Shalini, your pain of 10 months bore a fruit of pain for rest of our lives . Only once taoji uttered, " oi Rajinder, keep your cool and consider it to be the wish of almighty". That was the typical welcome of a girl child in most part of the northern India. In fact in modern time the same practice of thought continues to some extent.

Chapter-2

And…. another who had had cried out to bliss the whole family of Roychowdhrys on the same day of Shina's birth in the other part of the sub-continent. Being their youngest baby girl in the clan in the Comilla district of Bangladesh, Roychowdhrys were very happy.

The Roychowdhrys had a very efficacious image in the entire district of Bangladesh since the period of pre-British raj in the sub-continent. They had a possession of only 10 big bagans(orchards)of mango of 10 different breeds,7 bagans of jackfruit of various sizes, paddy land of 200 acres,6big dighis(lakelet). Aswini Roychwdhry and chanchala Roychowdhry were very blissful to have a daughter in their final consideration. They named her Renuka. Renuka was born to the purple. Since her very infancy she was very moody, filled with attitude but as soft heart as Shina's in the other part of the sub-continent. Renuka cared for all and respected all the elders. There in her khandaan (clan), Renuka was born carefree minded, naughty, playful and a sensible child. She was sentimental being the youngest and pampered. Before Renuka there were 10 brothers and sisters in the family. The immediate elder was just 1 year older, Sabi, friendly and as if her bosom friend of every moment. But the bitter consideration of Renuka's life has to swallow the dissection for ever from Sabi when she was 8. It was a severe fever of one night to end sabi. But everybody believed she had been carried away by one of their relatives who died in some mischevious star movement. Besides, she had expressed to Renuka before she dies, "…..look here goes our aunt in palanquin, she is calling me to go along with her". The dissection was very painful stroke to Renuka's tender heart.

The eldest of all was Hiralal Roychowdhry having an age gap of 35 years from Renuka. The brothers next to him was chinivai, mejhda and sunavai. In between Hiralal and chinivai two elder sisters another two sisters between chinivai and mejhda and after suna Vai more three sibblings including renuka the youngest. The bhavis(sister-in-laws) of Renuka were not much considering with the pampering girl Renuka, that she had from her brothers. Except one bhavi, who Loved and cared for her, she was her Mejhda's wife (mejo boudi).she was mere a kid of 8 or 9 when mejo boudi came into the Roychowdhrys. She too went to the groom party on the love chariots of three brothers shoulders and caring laps. querying all about the way and the brides. On the first view of Renuka her newly bhavi who too named renuka started pampering her and pulled her into love lap. "so, you are my lovely little sister in law, whom I've heard much from your mejhda. Renuka's mejhda had told a lot about her to the bride Renuka in their first meeting. Bride Renuka found her sister in law really to be a darling child of every one, who easily could possess the hearts. It is rightly said the first sight is all effective throughout your life and it ends with your last breath. Renuka had an extra ordinary prowess in angling, climbing trees, running, swimming…

While digging up potato from the field she helped her father and others in the course. She took it to be a game and felt a pleasure. Being very cute and innocent child, she would ask question all the time in the course of digging up; baba how many potatoes sprout from a single potato...? who will purchase these potatoes from us…? Why these potatoes are round in shape…? Many more such query from little girl made the field very interesting. She would also help the peasants with water and sweet words to them, which sooths them like tonic amidst scorching sun . Finishing all his busy task her baba would carry her in his shoulder to their home with sweets and lozenges to her. Her brothers were very sober, gentle and respected persons. They were all down to earth and humble.

Chapter-3

The 8th among the siblings suna bhai was very intelligent, bold and responsible shoulder in the family. He could led any trouble- some road like a smooth flow of water. He was man of vitality and could do the unpredictables. At his super youth he stood over almost 6 feet and around 150 pounds. He was the only person in the Roychowdhrys and even in the district to pass matriculation in the then east Bengal. His intellect could calculate massive sums in the murmuring lips and the calculation of land area in the fraction of minutes. so everybody used to call him weather small or respected senior, 'babu'. Accordingly, his neck was always out of zamindari function unlike others did in the family. Although he was out of all zamindari accounts, but was very social and participant in all sports events like, game of lathi, hadudu (kabaddi), swimming.

Once while returning from a village zatra(drama) it became late in night, he was with his friends toli(gang). Suddenly the dark jungle way sounds with the roar of a tiger. All were frightened and panic, but suna bhai bearing a lathi boosted confidence among all and advised all to walk closer holding each other. The time came when one tiger comes face to face of another. " So king you have approached to dine us ….. but you have to go for a battle with this tiger first…." That was the brimming confidence, all of a sudden… sunabhai blew his mighty lathi in the head of the tiger, receiving the mighty blow the tiger cleared the way mingling in the darkness. " O dear tiger you are so easily conquered, I cannot believe".

He was called for a govt. job and shifted to Agartala in Tripura(India)as a tehsildar. The senior Roychowdhry was against his decision. But getting the golden opportunity in hand sunabhai couldn't let it slip. Now the Roychowdhrys were splitting into two region Bangladesh and India. There was a very narrow line of split then. No body could have imagined of future separation from ones native. Sunavai joining his job moved to Comilla once in every weekend. The distance of his home to the place of posting was just a mile. Walking was preferred to any other communication. Sunavai took a house on rent first. It was the initial of

70's, All had a firm believe that Indo-Bangla would be a same land under the leadership of the then Indian PM. smt. Indira Gandhi rather to be called East Pakistan. Renuka and the elder daughter of chini vai were admitted to school in Agartala, supposing to have more facilities and better future career . Chini vai and mejhda also moved to Agartala to start a business together. Ultimately their wives for the sake of husbands and children needed to move with them. But mejho boudi remained with senior Roychowdhrys.

Chapter-4

The expectation of having Bangladesh as an Indian state was shed down with the 'Bongo-mukti-juddho movement'; Bangla got an independent identity from Pakistan in 1971.

The great lose had to pay by the Roychowdhrys, especially by the Aswinis. Other Roychowdhrys could sell or exchange their properties with the resident Muslims of north eastern India. But Aswinis couldn't manage either. They had to bear the prick of partition very sharp into their heart.

If apply our hawk eye there might be many such families to bear the common prick into their hearts. The sweet memories and the landscape of the "Sonar Bangla" (golden Bengal) blessed them to raise in life. The story of independence war, Bongo Mukti-Juddho, and the unity, honesty of the 'desher manush'(native fellow) were the frequent utterance of all the members of the family. In Agartala, whenever and wherever any fellow from native Bangla met coincidentally with chinivai or mejhda; they won't call them with their name , they would rather address them ' desher manus'. Whenever any known fellow drew together ; they would be called to their home, would ask all about their friends and the condition of their lands , property. Then they would start discussing about the heroic contribution of sweat and blood in the 'Bongo-mukti juddha'. Mejhda and chinivai would roar and pomp along with the fellow guests. " I was in the lathel (cane)group", chinivai Vai would say. Mejhda surpassingly would say, " I was leading the sword and spear Troup of our district, in fact the gorilla Troup was under my vision. Every mid of the night we assembled in the big open fields and arranged our fighters for the ' juddho'. Both the brother's breast would puff up.

But all such masculine talks persisted just only before sunavai enters the room. All would quell and scattered off the council.

Even after Bangla independence, the Roychowdhrys kept a communication with their huge estate or empire in Bangla. Now remains Aswini and Chanchala almost alone with some relatives, caretakers and darowaans(guards) to look after them and the property. Every weekend all the members in Agartala moved to Bangladesh, enjoyed and did serve their mother and mother in law. Chanchala also felt the days of weekend very entertaining and warm with all grand children, sons ,daughters and the caring of daughters in law. But every body knew that the days are just like sand in hand day by day slipping out of the fist.

Chapter-5

And the day came when they needed to shift to India night and day. The Muslims who served and worked all day and night being loyal to Roychowdhrys, started betraying and occupying the property slowly. Everyday something will happen but the hand behind such happening was an unknown mystery. Finally, one morning the peasant class started open betrayal with the muneem(accountant) of Roychowdhrys. They demanded to double their wage or they will not go to the fields. Opposing their view and vigour, muneem was assaulted and Aswini himself had to come in his rescue. He was very dissected of heart . In alone, sitting in his arm chair, swinging and recalling his past, " In your hungry days, I provided you with food and cloth, in your crisis I gave you work in my land, but with the turn of time you show me your red eyes, how mean the human world, how selfish you the man kind….." it was the last rainy season, when Abdul had a blown roof and shivering with his three children and wife; went to him and pleaded " hujur (my Lord)save my children, the storm has blown my home to kick me under the tree, save me", senior Roychowdhry's heart melts to shelter the bereaved family in his bungalow in the tyranny of horrible storm, and the very next morning his house got mend up. "…..Now that voice grudge upon me. All you seems demanding me to leave my home and property."

One night one of the granaries were lit into fire. It was the verge of extremity, so the senior Roychowdhry decided to move to Agartala. The house was barrened just keeping their faithful servant, Rahim in the big bungalow. Rahim was an orphan child, who just came up to learn his name, when he was borne by Aswini to his home. He was provided all his fundamental needs of normal life, food, cloth and what he needed for all comfort. Only couldn't make him a book lover. Rahim was affectionate to all and he himself loved to serve all like a loyal fellow especially Aswini almost in every task. He was then a young stout man of twenty five when the entire responsibility of the bungalow was given to his shoulder. He was so loyal to Roychowdhrys that although he was a Muslim yet no hesitation was in anybody's mind. Moving to Agartala a plot of land measuring a 'kani'(almost one acre) was purchased by Aswini. Upon the plot, a house made of tin was erected. It was quite comfortable for all Roychowdhrys to live together. Renuka and champa, the daughter of chini vai planted many flower plants and a small kitchen garden. The lawn was well grazy , the children played all day and afternoon there. The shadow of mango groves, the jackfruit trees, green paddy land and the estate of 200 acre are now shrinked into mere land of one kani. The zamindar era of Roychowdhry was vanished in cheap fate. Aswini Roychowdhry was pricked in his heart the trident of separation from the sonar Bangla, the big estate of forefather and the dignity and respect that he had empowered in the native land. He sat silent all day and night in his easy couch having the gold studded stick and the pipe of hookah in his lips. The white dhoti, and the white cloak with golden button in it, a gold frame of specs produced a stature of a perfect zamindaar. He was just an assimilation of a crownless king. He all day watched the children playing and shared his broken heart with her chanchala at evening " is this my fate of golden days…..chanchala? I wish my ill time had forsook me more couple of years….. I wish god had given all such days after closing my eyes". Chanchala just could pacify his turmoiled heart saying "our days are gone look at our children, they are adjusting and earning their own, be contented…..". she would sooth his feelings and press his legs to comfort.

This way half a year passed. The old Roychowdhry would stroll morning and evening, knowing no people of his age there.

Senior Roychowdhry supposed to be the king without crown, his stature in the stake, no admirer to bow before, no task in life, just to hide for ever. One day he took the plunge, that he cannot lead such a life of shrink as if in a cage; so he finally moved back to the bungalow of sonar Bangla . Putting up a massage to his sons before leaving Agartala for ever….. " important resolution related to my soul, I want to discuss with you all; kindly follow your respected baba once for ever…..yours baba". Getting such strong herald from their old father all the three brothers decided to meet him in their bungalow in Bangladesh.

The senior Roychowdhry assembled the entire family in the bungalow in sonar Bangla one fine morning and asserted his wish to stay at his own native land and remain there until

his last breath counts, " look you all my parts ,
you all are in fresh blood , in your state of
erudition, can erect your future, career,
establishment in your new adaptation, but this
old Roychowdhry is now in concluding stage of
all his role in the life drama. There is no hope of
new adaptation, and I can't live like a bare tree
for you all. I have my own esteem to keep
blowing and preserve ….. what would be the
future, I would be staying in my sonar Bangla".

whatever ill may happen to his
fortune he won't flinch a hair. He also invites if
any member wants to join him; none but
Chanchala being his umbra of life stayed along
with him. Aswini also understood the situation.
So he advocates the dissection of his sons… "
you have many reason to go in India and stay
there for your job and future, so my children
stay well there". From that very evening,
Aswini could sigh a relax, he felt very elated
from inside, " Chanchala now I am free like
ever, now I can feel the open air, and the
warmth of my forefathers…..". next morning
all the 3 sons moved to India.

Chapter-6

Roychowdhry took a very serious follow through over his entire estate, the mango grooves, the paddy lands, dighis, and oher bagans. Rahim escorted him all the time; he also informed him about the capturing of one of the dighis by the Muslims and doing fishing on it. " Not only this hujoor, some of the paddy lands have also been over taken by them and doing their own cultivation". Aswini asked, " Rahim did they try to harm you and haveli in any way?" very frighteningly Rahim uttered, " bade babu(my Lord) a couple of times I have been assaulted and threatened to leave the haveli for ever, quite a time I have been forced in the name of my religion, but I couldn't , as it's order of my master to look after roychowdhry's honor in Bangla until you returns….". Roy Chowdhry feels with tears in his eyes. He pulled Rahim into his heart and patted him "don't fear Rahim, now your bade babu is here and still alive". The very next morning the royal zamindaar took his bath did puja of maa shakti with aarti and offering flowers and praying for strength to an old single warrior…..it seemed as if he has tied his turban to regain his lost honor in Bangla. Wearing his zamindaari suit and the gold studded lathi called upon his muneem and sat in his big verandah of the haveli. He sent Rahim to call and arrange all Hindu lathels and pehlwans to the haveli. Within an hour all the muscle came to the zamindaar . Roychowdhry deployed them all around the haveli and the entire property. the dighi and the paddy fields. The vigour, zeal and the administration of a royal spirit of the zamindaar was the worth watching that exhibited. The zeal of 80 years aged was like a burning flame amidst the dark storm of partition. Now the muslim peasants were thrown out of the fields and other jobs.

A born tiger can never live in cage, he is the only king of the jungle, what hurdles or even death comes in his way he would fight till last breath and survive his honor of royalty. At the verge of life an old man without any support of sons and relatives fought for his Roychowdhry's ego and prestige. All over in Bangladesh, Hindus were brutally killed by majorities. Aswini knew well, his stand was just like challenge to an approaching cyclone. Aswini preferred death to surrender his fame in the hands of tyrants.

Still the Comilla district was little touched of the then brutality. The situation forced the sons to visit their parents frequently. Along with them Renuka always joined with her haughtiness. There she loved and pampered by her parents and sharing all the stories of her school and friends. Her father would giggle and kiss the sweet child. the series of meeting frequented for almost one year, but Roychowdhry never desired to go to India.

Chapter-7

Almighty favored Renuka's ill fate since her childhood. She was only 10 when she lost her father. The old tiger left all his pride and honor in a very fascinating manner for ever but with the flame of victory and royalty.

Renuka was on visit to her parents on school vacation in summer. She had no such sensation that her father was ill and went out with other children, her mother called her not to go any where but Renuka assured her mother not to go far. In the afternoon when little Renuka came back to home she found entire haveli was crowded with the villagers, in the middle her baba was lying covered. She was filled with awe, "maa what happened to baba?" almost cried the little eyes…holding a dozen of ripe and raw mangoes in her skirt. Her maa just hold her tightly and cried aloud, "your baba is no more" Renuka dropped down all the fruits and started pulling her father's hand…" baba get up baba, I'll not go any more to the mango grooves, nor for fishing alone, baba , o baba please open your eyes, I'll abide all your advices and do no more stubbornness for lozenge, I'll be a good child of you and maa". The words of small Renuka just brimmed the eyes of her mother and the entire crowd. She just follow the funeral way behind everyone crying and running uttering softly, "baba don't leave me, don't leave me….." The little hands rubbed the face of Aswini with love for the last time and bade him bye for ever, " wherever you go baba stay well and be a king". She ran back to her crying mother and tried hard to pacify her and sat in a corner of the room . After the cremation, the three brothers came back and stayed in Comilla for a month. Completing all the rituals they now got dissipated to get back to their earning land. Chanchala urged them, " if you all go back to Agartala , who would look after all the wealth of Roychowdhry? Who 'll take care of your old mother?"

" You are our mother, you procreates us, you cannot be parted, your care is our responsibility. So you are going to Agartala with us", said sunavai. " and our properties…..we 'll engage a caretaker and visit 'em every month", don't you bother dear maa" answered mejhda.

But to calm an old mother is not just enough to protect a huge estate . In fact the junior Roychowdhrys might have known what was the fate of their wealth in Bangladesh.

After the demise of senior Roychowdhry the scattered family couldn't maintain the legacy and moved to India for ever. The power of majority bound them to leave the huge empire unwillingly.

Chapter-8

The 2nd phase of Renuka's life started under the guidance of her bhavis. The chini bhavi showed all her strictness to Renuka but all considerate for her champa. Both were in the same class in school, of same age but preference first to champa. One day Renuka was playing with her toys very concentrated but the strict eyes of chini bhavi could hardly bear that, shouting she called Renuka " where is your study…..you dumb". Pulled her kicking all the toys of mud aside…" you'll have no food until you finish your task. On the other side champa is called out softly by her mother for lunch. Till afternoon Renuka cried and studied. The punishment was rescued by mejho boudi. Another day, Renuka went for bath in the near by pond, did little late to come out of water, the Hitler bhavi came on spot and caught the culprit red handed in the pond jumping and swimming and enjoying her way without noticing chini bhavi. When she came out she was pulled by her ear and slept in the chin all of a sudden. Instantly chini vai came into the spot he noticed all the happenings and took her wife in strong hand. Renuka was so fair complexioned and soft with round face small eyes thin lips, that may attract any body's pamper. The strong protest from chini vai for the first time alarmed chini bhavi in future regarding Renuka's look after. But that whole day Renuka did take no food and cried out silently at her small cot. In the evening, mejho boudi came to her as she knew no one but she can make her fresh of mood. She took Renuka in her lap and feed her tenderly. With smile Renuka slept in her bhavi's loving lap. Renuka was sharp and intelligent and always stood among first and second rank in the class, in the other hand champa could hardly pass her primary level. This made her chini bhavi more jealous. But in the standard 10 Renuka suffered para typhoid couple of times. This was another spear of ill fate upon Renuka to apart from her books for ever. Doctors in the second attack of para typhoid alarmed Renuka's brothers not to continue her study else she might be suffering of brain related problems. A few years later Renuka raised up to her beautiful youth. She had earned the prowess of knitting, painting, cooking, Stitching. It was in the mid 70s when Renuka lost her mother who was suffering from liver related problems. After few months Renuka got a coincidental marriage proposal. It was just all of a sudden. There was no hurry to look for her life settlement from her brother's part. The initial proposal for the marriage was for another girl from their near relative, but that girl was not prepared then for her settlement. She left for Calcutta to avoid the proposal. But the groom party arrived to look the girl and her family. It was a golden proposal the mejhda found to shift for Renuka, in this way they would not get insulted in front of the groom's . they managed to show their sister, in the first look Renuka was selected as the would be bride. Renuka too found the boy quite handsome to touch her heart.

Chapter-9

Then comes her next phase of her life. Renuka was knotted to a very handsome person, who was in full fledged youth worked in Indian Airforce, a sporting person, well maintained stature, very fair complexioned as if the blend of milk and apple. All were happy and found him to be the blessing of god for Renuka. The youth was named Jishu. The name of the person justly assimilated his nature and behavior. He was a vegetarian, speaks always straight in front but the truth. His eyes were bold against the injustice and soft as snow for the poor and sufferer. He had also a good legacy of forefather , the third son in the Sinha family his father was a colonel in army, having 4 sons from 2nd wife and one son and 2 daughters from the 3rd conjugal. Jishu had to move all around the country on service purpose. Thus Renuka too moved and learnt the art of varieties, different religions, customs, pulkari, pickle, cuisines, languages….. adaptability was her bench mark of character. She loved the humanity the most. She was just the sprinkle of holy water to human kind. Where only jealousy, show- off life style and unfair competition brooded among the so called social animals. These qualities were broadly visible in the feminine world of high rank holder of defense colony. She was loved by the most and yet envied by a few. In one year of her knot a girl child was blessed to the couple. She was having all the look of western mam sahib as the IAF quarters fellow regarded. " laxmi has come to your home Jishu, her whole appearance resembles the light of the goddess....." the friends and companions of Jishu used to say all the time. The wife of the station commander frequented very often to have the glimpse of the girl with rosy lips, and cheeks, and a complexion of snow white. She was earlier a good admirer of jishu for being the best sports person in the station, whether as an athlete, cricketer, a footballer. Jishu was all rounder. He performed good yoga as well. Now she has become the admirer of his daughter as well. The couple was very happy to have such a bright child to love the most. They named her Ragini. When she was just 2 years, she stammered to have brother for her as a play mate. The almighty too had such a similar planning to bless a complete family. And after one year of such desire from Ragini a baby boy born to them. It as a complete family. Sinhas were very happy to lead a comfortable life. Since childhood both the children were cultured up with all the manners of a royal family, way of communication, respecting and praying almighty, every morning and evening. Music, cycling, a full sort of curricular activities were designed by Jishu and Renuka for their lovely wards.

Renuka was very economical lady to maintain all expenditures, savings and even if any monthly salary of Jishu missed, no hurdles to the expenditures was faced on. Almost 12 years of smooth lovely path of life covered by the small family. There was lots of ups and downs in the journey of life. This one 'yuga',(12 years period) supposed to be the golden time of Renuka's fate. She might have been blessed only these few years in her life to cherish well.

Chapter-10

It was one struggle-some Saturday, that ushers the staggering and thorny way from smooth journey of life of sinhas . Jishu struggled hard all day for admission of both the children in an established convent school in the town. The couple dreamt of their children very lofty. Jishu once expressed to Renuka …. "my Ragini will be a doctor and Rituraj will be an engineer….. you see that our son would speak such a fluent English that the whole society would respect him praise him for his knowledge." Renuka smiles and prays almighty for the fulfillment of the dream of their life. Both the children all the time presumed to be already a doctor and an engineer. When Rituraj was just 7, the ceiling fan of their quarter was not working, need an electrician for repairing or to check out the problem. Ritu with all his guts and presumption of a born engineer took out a screw diver from the tool box and started opening the screws of the switch board. After screwing in and out hammering the parts in the box he switched on the fan and it starts rotating its wings well. Mother from kitchen comes to the spot and awfully looks at Ritu, "what sort of work is in your hand? Are you crazy?" but Ritu with pride; looks up at the fan and smiles at his mother. When Jishu came at noon from office, Renuka praised her son as an already engineer. Rituraj puffed up his chest more in pride. Then after he kept himself busy in all sort of mechanical tits and bits of home. In his 7th birthday Ritu demanded an aeroplane as his dream shifted to become a pilot. He collects a chopper and an aircraft all day long he would play with the toys seeming them to be real. One day Jishu asked in playful mood engineer has gone a pilot now. Cleverly Ritu replied taking a time " No baba this is an aeronautical engineer so …busy in his crafts" and both son and father would smile and laugh.

The cursed Saturday……. After struggling for school admission finally came. The most hectic day for Jishu and then he just paused himself in the chair at office at his section room. But suddenly one of his collegue burst out and ran towards Jishu… "Jishu what happened , why are you silent,…" the collegue just saved jishu of being fallen from the chair he was sitting. At once Jishu was carried into MI room of the airforce Guwahati Base. After completing initial care Jishu was shifted to medical college. Renuka was informed of the incident by one of the head nurse Mrs. Pal , who stayed in the same building in the hexagonal quarter to Jishu's. Renuka ran keeping every thing even her children upon the responsibilities of the neighbors. She was accompanied by Mr. Mazumder whose quarter was in the ground floor. Renuka went first to the MI Room and from there to the medical college on office vehicle. Ragini and Rituraj kept waiting without any meal but at evening news came from the hospital along with Mr. Mazumder that jishu needs to stay at hospital care and Renuka would have to stay along. One Mr. chakraborty, Mrs. Mukherjee, Mrs. Thakur, Mr. and Mrs.Mazumders and all others jumped all together to help the sinhas. The kids were looked after by the helping neighbors for next 3 days. Renuka took all information about the children from the hospital itself in fact she was reluctant. Although both the kids were having sleepless 1st night. When both saw their parents at home the blast of happiness was inexplicable. Rituraj took it to be a test of god, all is and all will be fine. From such a kid age Ritu could castle high believe about god. The test of time didn't stop yet Jishu had to have a bed rest for 1 and half months at home. In MC he was detected to have a stroke besides high sugar level. But the condition gets deterioted gradually. Mrs. pal every day pushed insulin in the afternoon. The quarter of Jishu remained full of visitors ,office colleagues, friends and neighborhood specially all time engaged In supporting Mrs. Sinha. All appeared to boost Renuka with confidence, support and promise to remain beside her hardship. In fact Renuka didn't know it was just a trailer of her future days of crisis. Around 14 days later Jishu could come round. In this 14 days Jishu had to pass at a local nursing home at Paan Bazar in Guwahati. Almost three months of health breakdown Jishu came round fresh. Anyways, the crisis of health is meagre in compare to motherland. There arises a crisis in the border kashmir and the base Airforce from Guwahati needed to post Jishu in the border along with his Wing. This was the devotion of a pious lady to lord and husband that could generate the vibration of fresh energy into Jishu. Passing the days of test at the Kashmir ghati Jishu came back very pompous at Guwahati base. He feels great relax and contentment seeing the blooming face of children, who ran to the glimpse of their father.

Chapter-11

" Baba ,o dear baba, why do you go leaving us away?"… Rituaj cries and uttered.. "you don't know how lonely we feel and maa keeps crying and remain tensed without you ". The kashmir ghati was pacified by the Indian army with the assistance of Indian Airforce not less than 3 months.

After passing horrible days of gun battles, and air bombing preferred for a refreshment, so took a trip along with the family to Agartala at Renuka's brothers house. There they passed around 1 month, meeting all the relatives with sweet memories and warmth. There Jishu was treated as jamai raja but more as a nation's hero. He went to his own land, at north Tripura as well and met all his side relatives .

Coming back to Guwahati A/f station almost passed six month, every thing was going in good pace . Rituraj and Ragini had good scoring in their school finals. The memory of the tour they repeated all the time and a hope aired always to go for a next tour next year. Ritu would count days for next vacation. But the wheel of fate wishes something different almost after six months of return from the tour in the month of June Jishu had a cardiac attack and needed to admit nursing home and then to Guwahati medical college. Renuka's sunavai and his sons arrived on hearing the crisis of Renuka. Suna vai just appeared like Sri Krishna on time to help a poor sister. Suna vai and his two sons for one month did to and fro to hospital and home. Seeming just a bit better they prepared for back to Agartala….. " dear my sister now I have to move back.. my leave from job is over.. Choton is also having his exam of higher secondary"…. But Choton and Madhav stayed to help the aunt. " papa u move alone to Agartala, we will be here with dear aunt until our uncle comes back".

One day Renuka says…..Madhav and Choton " now your uncle is getting round so you both go to your place and do your tasks". So unwillingly they moved back leaving their aunt upon the quarter's companion.

Renuka didn't want them to have, to help her leaving behind their important tasks at Agartala.

Chapter-12

But the primary pain to struggle the hard days was all upon Renuka's shoulders she had to go 60kms away from Airforce station, managed children and school, cooking for them as for Jishu. Being a lady it was a very challenging period which she performed very responsibly. No rain could bar a wife, no scorching sun could Pierce the confidence .

Once she was severely injured in a heavy shower. That was a heavy shower Sunday, no bus was available from A/F area. To fetch a bus she had to go for 25 km. at Maligaon; from there she could get any vehicle for medical college. She got ready for her 'tirth yatra'(pilgrimage), where she would meet her soul mate though in ailing bed. At the bus stop she waited and waited for long 1 hour in heavy shower, but no bus to board her on. At that moment she murmured " oh my lord, help this poor child to help her ailing husband, who is waiting for her care and company…..". really her lord at once accept the prayer. A neighbor with motor bike was going somewhere, he stopped and enquired "hello Mrs. Sinha…..how is our dada and why are you drenching?" He progressed towards her voluntarily. Renuka was quite confident to get the neighbor. She expressed all her situation. The fellow was ready to help her about and gave a lift up to Maligaon on his bike. But the test of time still on wait for Renuka. Almost reached at Maligaon, the bike skid in the wet road and the skid threw both the riders. The helping fellow didn't get much on his body but Renuka had a deep scratch and serious bleed in her elbow and calf. Yet not stopped there, neglecting her own wounds, she asked the fellow, " Sameer are you okay? See for my cause you hurt yourself badly". The fellow managed his bike and assured Mrs. Sinha of his well being. Even the bike had not a little damage on it. Renuka remained thankful to Sameer who led almost half of her destiny in such a wretched day. " Boudi, now you might get a bus from here, else I can go along up to hospital…" Renuka thanked him " no brother this help is too much for me". Sameer u move back but very cautiously. Renuka board a bus and moved for her 'tirth'. Again a small incident happened to her, while down board the bus near the hospital she stumbled and skid front of the stairs and adds more to her scored injuries earlier on the day. Finally she reached to the bed of Jishu. Jishu sighed a relief seeing her.

"Today so delay…" said jishu very emphatically. " No, actually bus is very short today and I needed to shift couple of buses and auto straight from VIP road". But now I'm with you…" said Renuka smilingly. Then she engaged herself in preparing Jishu's diets and medicine. That night she stayed at hospital.

Next morning when she came back to home, Rituraj ran to her, she was found little uncomfortable and as if unmindful to him. "What, What happened maa, is everything ok?" "Yes beta nothing to your worry" replied mother Renuka.

"But I can see your painful face maa". "Please tell me what happened?" now Renuka tries to lighten the situation… "Oh little scratch I got in my legs that's it". " show me maa" now Rituraj became very stubborn. When Renuka couldn't ignore her son she herself astonished to see her injuries and big scratches and black stained blood at her legs and shoulders. Rituraj screams "maa"and hugs his mother. Renuka first-aided and visits her doctor on that date next couple of days she stayed for a little rest.

It was her unflinching love and devotion for God and her husband that could bring jishu back to home after 45 days. Rituraj reveals all the incidents and struggle, her mother faced on that rainy day, and how he along with her sister spent lonely days without mamma and Papa. " you bleed your hands and legs, you did all for me, but didn't tell or shared any pain with me...!" uttered Jishu. " it's my duty to do everything possible for you, you need not to think for me, I am all okay from health and mind; and it's your time to get back very soon" replied Renunka very carnally.

Jishu was weak of health so he was considered from the office of the station Commander. He needn't to regular his office. In these days of crisis sunavai thought to send Ragini at Jishu's house in North Tripura under the care of his elder brother.

Days of high and low tides were passing desperately. It was almost 6 months after returning from GMC, the day was Maha shivratri..... everywhere, devotees were offering their puja, bhakti song, aarti and other preparation was adding colour to the day. In the other hand Jishu was suffering with a gas formation in stomach for 3 days. That night at around 2.00 the gas blockage gave no chance to Renuka to give a fresh fight against 'yama', the God of death. But Almighty had sent her brother and his two sons early on the very evening for her rescue. They we're from their tour of north India and was on a visit to Renuka.. on return.

Almighty ultimately blessed Renuka with all her hard effort for long two years. At midnight the cry and hue of Renuka awoke Rituraj, who goes near his mother and touches his baba and asks his mother very softly, " why are you crying maa? Baba is cool and well, his fever for last one day is cured now". In reply, Renuka shrieks, "no more baba, can you call, he has left us for ever…" yet small Rituraj could understand hardly, he ran to the Lord's 'ashana' and prays as soft as snow, " oh my Lord, please help my mother to stop her crying, please bring my baba back to his normal health… please help us…. Stop maa's painful tears". Again ran to next room and tries to pacify his poor maa. But he was removed from the site by sunavai to his bed.

Renuka could very hardly make her mind and heart calm. But the zeal, spirit and confidence all were brutally carried away from her now. No sign of extra virility remained in her, she realized and maintained silently the ill fate of a child, a girl, and a lady; these can't be wiped out with any effort, this is the signatory from the heaven. Yet the face of small Rituraj pushed her up; to move in life.

Chapter-13

Sunavai bears the family to Agartala at his home voluntarily, when the in-laws of Renuka showed no interest to help the poor family. Ragini was just 13 and Rituraj was 10 and Renuka just a lady of 33.

The smiling face of Renuka of Roychowdhary's was baked off in the scorching heat of the time you say or one can say fate. The tormented days are waiting more.

At Agartala, 3 brothers ,Madhav, Ganesh and Choton, had lost their mother at very young so were very happy to have Renuka and treated her like mother. They were very confident of their all round security of a mother . Renuka too looked after the home, sunavai and three nephews very carefully besides her children.

In the other part of the sub-continent — shina , the little Punjabi girl grew up with all compression from brothers and other elderly of the family. " Shina , aree o Shina, go and fetch water from the well, it's time to act your body", sound will come from an unknown room of the havelli. "Shina beti, go get my hukkah", the old man in the haveli would shout out. Some sounds " shina ki bacchi, who would iron my shirts?" with rough and harsh voice would address the poor girl.

Three of her brothers , cousin and taoji, taiji all exhausted her simplicity to end extend. Three brothers could carry their study up to intermediate and class tenth standard. One of her cousin moved to Delhi for higher studies related to hotel management course.

Shina though not sent to school, being a liability of the family yet the in-born quality or god gifted virtues produced such a loving and respected stature since her childhood. She did worship after taking bath and before starting other routine tasks. She helped her mother in cooking, spreading red chillies,pickles in the sun. Then she would care for cows and goats, goes to the bazra field would sing and plough and sickle along with other labour and relatives in the season . She also maintained a kitchen garden that was set by her aunt(taiji).

One morning, a cow entered and destroyed the kitchen garden. Taiji burst in fury, she called out

, " Shina, o Shina, o the curse one where are you? The cow is munching all the dhaniyas (coriander plant) tomatoes in the garden". Shina was fetching water in the pot from well, she dropped down the pot and ran to the spot. She pulled the cow out of the garden and tied it to the knot. Taiji beats her bitterly. The poor innocent girl of 16 cried all the day , that day she was even not called for lunch. Later, her mother brought the thali(meal) and tried to console her to take her meal. The poor Shina ate and slept silently. She shivered whole night and sobbed herself, how could an aunt be so rude and a mother so casual towards a child. Her mother thought to knot her conjugal life with kartar Singh, a robust fellow of their village. Kartar was a son of the village sarpanch, a powerful stature.

Chapter-14

But the fate of Shina was to steer something different.

An highly educated guy of their village named Shasikant Kaur once saw shina singing in the field, that mesmerized his mind with Shina's smile and innocent appearance. Shasikant had just returned from City completing his graduation. His father was also a very famous personality of the village, around 100 acre wheat and bazra land was in his name. Shasikant founded a primary School in the village with the help of his father and started teaching small kids of farmers and peasants. He was with a generous motive to literate the village children and uplift their status from thumb impression, tyranny of land Lords and money Landers. Shina too liked and impressed by his activities, manners and wisdom. Once or twice he went to Rajinder Singh's house to discuss some important issues related to his new mission of literacy in the village. Shina and shasikant had a few interaction by these visit. Besides sometime they also met at the big open ground where, Shina and her friends played,swinged and danced. Regularly Shasikant was found to move shanties of needy and effete, providing them with food, clothes, books and all generosity. While both the hearts crossed each others but could speak no words only eyes coupled. Sashi noticed one more thing in Shina's regular activities, she had a habit of purchasing lottery ticket of Punjab state lottery. In number it was just one ticket. While sipping cup of tea in the market site tea stall Sashi would notice her regular .

A soft feeling emerged into both hearts. Gradually, two hearts blinked red and became one single. They committed to stand together for whole life, in every situation whatever it may be. One morning kartar Singh saw the two loving hearts in the bazra field, hand in hand very happy to share each other's time. The romantic couple were not aware of the world around them, they were just swaying in their own world….. " look the rhythm of the green field coupled with the wave of the wind… the sun shine, birds singing, ….. these all are blessing our bonding for ever" said Shasikant very softly in the ear of Shina. Shina just hugged him and blushed. In the next moment after a silence "what do you do with lottery tickets Shina?" asked Sashi with a mocking tone. " Do you want to be a lakh pati?... O not pati, patni?"….. He giggled. Shina felt shy and replied smilingly, "look Sashi babu I am an illiterate and dependent Arcadian who only does domestic work efficiently. Besides who knows if someday I win a huge sum against a penny". " I've seen you spending money every day" said Sashi. "yes since my child hood I'd buy a ticket regular from my saved money given to me occasionally by my parents. This is my only hobby or expenditure. And I'm confident some day I'd be a very rich lady of self money". " ok dear, from your wealth could I 've some share for my self?" mocked Sashi. "No I won't give you a single penny, you teaser" Shina blushed.

No body knew this wealth or lottery would bring Shina's life climax.

Chapter-15

That Very day, while going back to his home on bicycle,Sashikant was hurdled by the greeneries of the bamboo park . There kartar tried to bully Sashi, " you go very romantic in the bazra field….." that's none of your business to follow….. you cheap" replied Sashi very straight. " The Rajinders are willing to give Shina's hand to me, so that becomes my business to follow on my would be wife, I don't like to see my girl with any other fellow alone, and that too in the field", Kartar alarms Sashi. Sashi clearly asserted his intension to Kartar regarding Shina, and also informed Shina's love for him. Two flame heats up in two hearts, one of love and caring and another of hatred and avengeful.

The nature cherished and nurtured the two very beautiful hearts very tenderly. Many moon lit evening Sashi and Shina met and shared very touchy moments.

One moon lit evening" Sashi the upper sashi cools the tortured trees and grass; animals and birds soothes the earth and grains in the field;

how mesmerizing and pacified the ground we are sitting". Shina uttered very warm, " similarly my Sashi soothes all the prickly attitude of my family, torturous trend of relations ..... you know no one cares my heart ,my pain, my wishes...... this world is supposed to be a baked earth of summer of our village and your love and care is just nature's spring watering this barren land". Shina sobs closing her eyes with her hands. Holding firmly the two hands of Shina , Sashi replied " you are as soft as a lovely Rose and as carnal as a pigeon.....my search was you to be my better half. The love and your company would be my shade in this scorching world. Shina you know my mission in the village, my dream related to this backward villagers, I need your love and support, I want to make them my fuel to lit up the light of knowledge and modernity here". The bubbly clouds breeze to comfort the loving birds.

The next day sun lit very rudely. The face of the sky gloomed with dark clouds all around. The heavy shower breaks down and all works in the field, all works in the market, all the customary duties in front of the bungalow of Rajinder came to halt. On the other side shina was enjoying the rain at her room through the open windows; running up to the roof singing, dancing all the day.

The rain poured to water the plants of love in human hearts. Contrary the rain brims the river to flood over the green fields, gardens, sway down the huts and hopes of simple people.

Chapter-16

That very rainy day Evil built up the nets of conspiracy in the rusty mind of kartar Singh. He felt himself to be a damn loser, from whom Shina is going into the arms of Shasikant. He cannot hear much about the love birds in the village, his eyes cannot imagine Sashi and Shina together. He gulps couple of patiala peg and determines to clear off Sashi from his way to Shina.

Kartar along with some of his evil mates planned to block Sashi by the bazra field. While returning back home from his social work, spreading light of hope , inspiration and future shining village in eyes even in the deadly weather. There happened tussle among kartar's paltan(gang) and Sashikant. Being a fearless punjabi, Sashi exhibit his vigour and Herculean heart before evil.

 The dark night cleared off with the glittering sun next morning. But into it's darkness Sashi also sank down. The gayful heart of Shina never dared to bloom again.

The next morning when the disappearance of Sashi aired through out the village all his family members, friends and villagers looked for Sashi everywhere through out the day, but no trace could they find. without a grain of food in mouth Shina too prayed almighty all day. But all went into vain.

"oh my lord….. a little elixir of hope and light in the dried up heart even, not bored in your just world!"

The life of Shina throws the light upon an ill-fated soul in this earth. Her character reveals…..; there in this universe nothing good is stable or achieved for long. The ' kaal chakra',the wheel of Time, even speed up their good span of time. These soul are just sent to bear the thorns of life although they air sweet fragrance of humanity in their environment.

Years passed on, Shina's flowery face and Rosy heart now shrinked as if thorns, dried in beaming and scorching sunshine of fate. Her parents left one after another, and now she remained at her home very lonely among her brothers and cousins. She always kept her day busy in bazra field and evening in painting, cooking looking after her niece and nephews. She smiled in the crowd. When slept at night cried bitterly for her love Sashi. " you promised to stay by me, I will be your inspiration, village would be a place of love and knowledge in every mind, but where are you my heart? My heart bleeds for your love, when 'll I meet you? If you are not in this world call me up, my eyes are still looking for you just like- partridge looks for the moon".

Quite a time the evil heart, Kartar tried to gain her in youth but her heart wore the 'chola'(dress) of a widow; and decided not to knot any more with heart with anybody.

Finally the bell rang which is supposed to be the conclusion of a pious soul the end phase of Shina's life.

Chapter-17

Sashi left her, Shina now just carrying her life with the sweet memories and the mundane habits to keep herself engaged and veil herself from the pain.

She continued her habit of purchasing a lottery ticket from Bazar. Ultimately the perseverance bore fruits. Shina won an amount of rupees ten lakh. She didn't know whether to cherish or just think it to be a normal phenomenon in poor life.

She yammered, " O Sashi, this amount would have been for your dream school in our village. I'd love to see all your dreams full filled; how hoity- toity would have been from you to me. I miss all the moments darling. But I still can do something for your dream to cherish, you just support me from heaven. I'll contribute whole the amount to build a school in our village.

 Entire village now look at Shina as if a boon from above. Some started calling her 'sethaniji', some addressed her 'Malkin'. She became nearer to a celebrity. A woman of means.

Her family members now started oiling Shina in their own ways. She became eye candy for them. She presumed such cunning act of her family. So she flinched all such manners. All desired to grab the money from Shina. Most desirous were Ranjit and rajveer. They became ambitious to own whole of the lottery amount.

Ranjit Singh appeared to his sister and asked very politely, " dear sister I congratulate you on your big win. In fact we are proud of you". Shina glare with no emotion and searching out the root cause of such modus. " sister you see ,we are facing a huge loss in our agricultural production. Market is very down for wheat and bazra this year, a huge amount of debt is dued to clear off bank. This is a blessing of God we can say that you 've won the lottery amount of ten lakh rupees", said Ranjit and rajveer just adding smile and asserting Ranjit.

"I'm going to give not a single penny for your business and losses", affirmingly said Shina , " this whole amount is already fixed to donate an NGO to establish a school in our village and help the uneducated children".

"So you're not bothering your money with us",Rajveer screamed, "then you'll be dumbed of property share of Singhs, mind that, then you would go and stay in your school". "Sorry brothers, what harm you want more upon me I don't care about. But no penny would be spent other than the school establishment".

Shina contributed all the lottery money to an NGO related to education and welfare of backward people. She was limelight of newspapers and became an honourable lady in the village. The state government awarded her ' the best citizen samman' in fazilabad district of Punjab.

All these acts and achievements reddened the eyes of Singh brothers. After a long period of time smile of contentment brimmed in Shina's lips. She could talk with Sashi in heaven as if he too was happy and Cherishing the dream accomplishment of both. " I've done it dear, I wish you were beside me and share the precious award and honor of your toil and initiation". Shina cried looking high above in the sky.

Chapter-18

The ultimate plot of Shina's mortal play initiated with the distribution of the property among brothers. All decided to grab own shares with golden part bereafting old Shina from a penny. All took her to be a burden and unused utensil among them. Shina could demand only a small space for her remaining life and a piece of field, so that she could sleep at night and keep herself engaged to forget all her life. She simply urged her brothers " where would I go if you all push me out of my home? I beg you all not to be so harsh and unkind, I 'll not interfere any matter of you. Just let me stay here in small space ". The brothers all time cursed her like anything. They along with their wives decided to send her old age home in urban site. But why Shina wanted to stay back at village is untouched and unexpected one. Shina never wanted to leave behind her memories with Sashi, there in bazra field and mango groves. The matter of conflict continued for many days.

One dark night the two brothers of Shina conspired along with evil kartar Singh to finish the 65 years old shina for accomplishing their greedy wish. " Kartar, Shina is very possessive about her share of property, you know she is just like a bone in our throat now , we need to remove her completely. Would you join us in the mission to accomplish", asked Ranjit very ambitious. The mischievous Kartar paused for a while and uttered, " what is my benefit to help you brothers? Moreover you know once she was my crush. So how could you expect me to help you in your intension? "I know Kartar you very well", said Ranjit, " you are such a fellow who doesn't do anything without any self benefit, look this is the time to avenge your crush failure. And don't you worry, I've decided to give you a good share of bazra land in your name". Kartar jested and said, " I've been hurted very much from that Shina, I cannot forget the pricks given to me by her and Sashi long back. This is a golden offer that I can hardly let go. So my friends share me your Blue print of your planning". The party of mischievous motive well fueled by drinks up to late at night.

Now it's time to execute the plan . They abducted poor Shina while she was returning back from bazra field in the evening. The mischievous hearts planned to abduct her out of the state far enough from anybody's touch. At first they made her unconscious. At around 11.45 pm the mail from Punjab to Kolkata was reserved for four persons. Then from Kolkata they hired a Pvt. car up to Darjeeling.

Chapter-19

The mirror image of Shina in the east doing and performing all her responsibilities towards her two kids and for her brother, who gave her umbrella of support in the crisis of life. Without a life partner at very young age along with the responsibilities of two innocent children, could only hid her all pains, dreams and agony with mild smile, thanking heartily to God and her brother, accepting all as her fate to adopt and sway along with the time. Never did she expressed her pain and inner loneliness even to her children and supported fully with hard day-today activities at her brother's house. Assuming this is the only job she is sent for. To look after others even at the cost of her own happiness, she felt a bliss in serving others, despite any despair to self. Every thing was taken for granted in the course of the widow's life. She accepted all the reasons why her in-laws are unable to support her and her kids after Jishu's demise; she accepted regardless the proposal from her responsible and just brother, who had just expected the responsibility that would be taken by the Sinhas in the crisis of

Renuka's life after Jishu. Anyways besides all these Renuka accepted it too, that a young plant can hardly grow properly under the canopy of a big tree. She moved on with the only faith of her lord.

Ragini got married at her last teen with a very prosperous businessman, although she had a wish for completing her higher studies and go for a job. But this may be the effect of the say of Renuka.....' a young plant can hardly grow well under a canopy'. Being a sheltered under the responsibility of her brother and his family, she always remained alarmed from her and her children side so that over burden upon sunavai may not be added. Ragini remembered when she was a child, she only talked and dreamt of becoming a doctor. When ever she was asked what will you be in future..... instant reply came from a small girl, 'doctor'. Her father too tried to water her spirit of strong future... " yes you are my doctor and Raj will be my engineer". In this utterance a sigh of brimming joy and feeling appeared as if they had already become. "But now" she cried, "all, all went into vain, nothing is according to ones will. Only a rare fate survives with successful will and vision in this earth and they are super charged."

Rituraj, struggling all the way, stretching from school studies till his master's, Ritu didn't go for any private tutor. Although there were so hardship in his academic career. His mother and uncle(sunavai) asked him several times, "look you are in English medium school and all the subjects are not in our course of understand, so to do a good result in school level you need a few teachers". But looking at his mother's poor income from family pension and huge burden of responsibility upon his uncle for them, he just pacified their concerned advice, "you both need not to worry, I'm well equipped with my confidence to ease all my subjects and clear my school level. No private teacher is required for me. I'll add more and more effort into my studies". Whereas his fellow friends were having couple of teachers for a single subject. He vapoured her trouble at the smallest measure of his assumption, cleared the academic study with distinctions prepared himself for a better career, though that could not be the dream career of his childhood, which was encouraged by his father. Moreover Ritu started to earn since his academic career by providing pvt. tuitions, so that his expenditure of study and other things could be borne by himself. Ritu got couple of good jobs in govt. Dept. ,But he preferred to join an MNC, as he loved adventure rather than a comfortable way, whether it is his career, study or any relationship.

After getting a career, he took her mother out of over responsible life to a relaxed sphere. He tried to offer all sorts of comforts which she deserved. Settling the life of three sons of her brother into conjugal world, she felt her self relieved of her responsibilities towards her brother. Although sunavai didn't agreed Rituraj to get separated. Later he understood the situation demanded so. After a few years sunavai left this materialistic world suddenly. Renuka became very upset and felt as if abandoned with any guardian now, finding her son to be all for her. Her concern for God and religious crave and devotional activities got more compiled. Basically she was a holy hearted and a solemn soul. Opted veg, always supported honesty, never hurt anyone, straight forward in self exposition but mild and gentle.

Feeling too much for mother, her son Rituraj thought to gift his maa dream home and a daughter in law, rather a friend and a daughter, who can accompany her always, specially when he is out of station on job tour. So he moved to his Gurudev's ashram along with his maa and earned blessings for his ingress into the conjugal life.

There he received broad view of selecting a bride. Before the ceremony, Raj thought of owning a house first, so he looked for many plots, but the 'kaal chakra', the time cycle had prefixed some other story. " maa lets' have a new member at our life, she would be helpful to my spirit and also a support to your empty times. What you say maa?" Raj asked Renuka, in reply Renuka just uttered "all your wish beta, do what you feel the best".

And thus the wedding was conducted very pompous, relatives, gifts, dances, all rituals, it was a remarkable occasion in the family and in the entire locality. The bride was as per the search from Raj. Renuka too was happy to see her son's life is getting settled. Richa, the bride was too fair and simple.

Chapter-20

But the wheel of fate had dedicated something different and something that had never been expected in the night mare of Renuka. No body knew whose evil eyes fell upon the small and lovely family. The well started journey of new life halts in the sixth months, when the mental balance of the bride waved for some unknown reasons. It was taken that she might have made her mind to dissect a son from mother; all the phase of action from her day today thoughts, conversation meant to be that; despite she was loved and cared by Renuka and her husband and all other in-laws relatives. Even she could find no reason of her behavior. Richa was so aggressive to possess her husband , " You give me more time, I don't want to be ordered and follow your mother very much in my life". She won't listen being a new member which she ought to do. One night she reached her extreme and dared to stifle Raj in the midnight. But when she was caught safely it's found that as if she had been possessed by some unknown power. Many doctors were being visited but no final conclusion appeared. Medicines just made her health deteriorated.

This is only firm believe in God by Renuka and some good deeds of Raj and Richa, the bride got relieved of all mis-happenings with her. Now the track of life starts once again rolling. The family of three members always tried to deal with other's welfare and serving the needy and poor . They moved to Gurudev's ashram together to earn blessings for new innings of good life. All pray to have love, respect and healthy relationship in life and have the full permanent desire and zeal to serve their lord.

But the written verse from heaven was something unorthodox.

Chapter-21

From the ashram the three moved for a fresh to Darjeeling. There the sprightly tour was well on for a revival of life journey. The mountain sights, springs, the tea gardens and floral views, temples all were enchanting the old night mares of passed moments of conjugal life.

Returning home a feeling of freshness dwelt in their spirit, in their relationship. The ode to spring in rustic life of Renuka seems to be shined. But as said in this earth creature also born to live a suffering life. There are people like shina and Renuka do well for others ever, but in return you only expect despair, suffering, even your fundamental basic life is also in strife. An unknown or anti move of clock falls upon Renuka. It's always heard that after strife and struggle the phase of relief and pomp blends in ones life. The Shina's fate was abducted and Renuka's to be.

The discipline and pious life of Renuka starts suffering of health. An unknown cause gave much short duration to Renuka and her son to subdue the strike of time, being puzzled running everywhere seeming and believing in God over head for all good. It was complete unexpected stand of their love life, Rina closes her eyes for ever. Although her eyes had couple of dreams to be fulfilled. Many more tasks and happiness that she deserved in this earth of god remained half completed. She did want to live a while for a relish of good time which she had never believed of her any time. How could god bring down such a cruel fate for such a pious soul? Is this not an injustice with the soul of Renuka? Her son strived all for his mother very hard only good of his mother was soul desire but the entire universe round anti clock with deaf ears and heart.

Rituraj remained zipped off mind and starred at his Best friends, who were since he lost his father and from whom he earned lot of support in test time of life. Raj always supposed his Best friends are sitting high above his head and fate to steer his life as per it's need. His heart always puffed up with their unseen presence. He just starred at them, and asked within,…

" since I lost my father, I lost my childhood,I lost my little heart' s soft desire and the infancy, my study, my dream, my initial way of life all doomed to despair, only struggle and hardship of minute time entangled to lead through black holes of life only one hope… my maa is with me, full filling her wishes I would erase all my despair and pains of life. Only her smile wheeled me ahead and your shadow soothed me to bestow, then why my friend….. the only wish of my life kicked so hard that now I can't stand to accept with ease your presence. All that I thought of you… were my Mirage…..? why I am still searching light of my innocent wish and that my initial feeling, that the presence of my Best friends are absolutely true…..". many such questions in Raj unruffled him and followed the funeral of his maa sobbing and kissing her forehead for the last time, which he did always before sleeping at night.

Chapter-22

Raj had had a firm believe that if anything you desire, you pray and do whole heartedly, you definitely blessed from the good spirit of the entire universe; even almighty has to bestow if that is replete with pure love and respect.

It was the love and respect of a mother and a father, that compelled Lord Krishna in 'Dwapar yuga' to bring back Punardatt from the sackle of the god of death, 'yamraja' after a long gap of time. He cannot bear the dissection of love , when the love is sanctified, it definitely convince even the almighty to disprove the move of the time wheel.

Rituraj had only his darling mother in this mortal world whom he supposed to be his own part of being, rather him of her. He always took an extra care and looked for every sort of her comfort. He never could have sleep seeing his mother gloom; never could he utter any harsh with her; even any time he impelled to, in the next moment he begged off her. He never could think his being in this earth without her. And he knew his God too never wanted that a son's love for his beloved mother would go into vain at any cost. What ever hurdle may comes on the way of a son but remain United with his mother even death, that even might be surpassed with the blessings of the almighty.

Chapter-23

Abducted Shina was brought to her end very cold blooded by her brothers and kartar Singh. They planned to erase any of the evidence to finish Shina. So Punjab to Darjeeling the mischievous hearts came bearing the innocent Shina unconscious in a cab. At a moment her brothers felt pity for Shina and thought to leave her at Darjeeling free. The three devil hearts sitting in a 'dhaba' sipping cups of tea chatting very seriously, whether to finish or not the poor Shina. By that chance the unconscious Shina wake up with a thunderous strength in the cab and slipped out very silently to fling far from the reach of the murderous people. When the three confirming Shina's fate, reached to the door of the cab with the intension to finish for ever the poor Shina. Their eyes remained wide opened to find Shina was missing in the darkness. They searched like demented but of no success. They stayed at Darjeeling for next couple of days to trace out Shina but could gather no hints in the hill station. Meanwhile Shina took refuge at a church on that very night. She became so week that could walk further and lost her conscious once again. The next morning the father of the church found the poor lady and sprinkled her mouth and eyes with water. When the father asked her where about and who she was, Shina recited all her story how she came there and begged the father to give her shelter and save her life. Father exclaimed with big sigh, " My child this is the home of God and you must be protected, you need not to worry here". Besides she was taken to one of the known person of father, Joseph,who was very kind and generous. There she was availed with medicines, food, and some clothes. Shina took a good sleep and rest for the day. Father took her care very meticulously. Joseph was informed to be alert if any Punjabi fellow, who may ask about Shina. The evil hearts searched and asked about Shina every where at Darjeeling but finding no trace they moved back to Punjab. Very grave hearted they returned and wishing to see no Shina there in Punjab. But a fear of reappearance remained in their hearts. So they tried to find out and hired some locals of Darjeeling to give any information about Shina any time if they get. By that time they also did to and fro to Darjeeling very often. Almost one and half year passed the incident happened.

Shina became very hail fellow of the hills. But the fair time of Shina's second phase of life seemed to come end. The hired informer of Kartar Singh got the glimpse of Shina there at the church area and among the locals. He instantly called his boss in Punjab. The half done mission to be accomplished by the three mischievous hearts. They moved fierily to Darjeeling the very next day and planned to trace off Shina's life for ever. Kartar and company tracked the way of Shina and found her to shelter at Joseph's house. In the mid night they enter the tethered house from back door and abducted Shina , this time they did no mistake and took her into deep jungle. Shina begged off them and affirmed that no harm would be propelled from her on the share of their property. " but I don't want to take any risk of future, and my dear sister you need to go now" vigorously laughed the two brothers and kartar added to them. The poor pray of Shina couldn't touch the cruel hearts and they finish her of her life. Pushing her down the cliffs of Darjeeling, " bid you good bye dear" sighed long the brothers.

Chapter-24

The wheel of Time stops there to take a halt and waits to move again. The soul of Shina taken very carnally into the lap of almighty. And Renuka found, while reaching to the abode of yamraja, the place which seems to be the land of dream. No pollution, no din and buzz, fair disciplined people all around, all are very serious on a queue progressing towards a person supposed to be the master of the land, the fate decider and the holy record personnel of all deeds, that is 'karma' of mortal people, in the 'yam lok', known by the name of Chitragupt sitting beside the crown. Renuka when approached near the Dias of the crown, Chitragupt computed repeatedly and found the wrong time of Renuka to be brought above. He found many tasks and responsibilities of mortal world and good deeds to be accomplished by her in future years. Now it has become a double deck burden of Yam Lok officials to retire Renuka once again to the earth with a proper match of timing and situation.

The heart of a mother too oppugn the chair of 'yamraja'. At the next moment she prayed, sought from the core of her heart to release her to reach her son.

" O! master of death, my son is very poor without his mother, he will ruin himself slowly and gradually, I know he can think nothing freely without me in life. His flourish would be rusted. O my master do you want to abrade a mother loving son so easily. I also know some mistakes might have been done by me and my son and that's why I'm here untime, but silly mistakes may not costs true love of a mother and a son departed. Being the master you cannot prefer such a balance of libra. We two have suffered many hard times of life but together we could win over, only with the believe, a little strife, a little more for a sure and definitely blessing future on earth. How can my soul go peace, seeing the turmoil and tormented life of my son? I still do have and remain my faith alive for my almighty and you. My Master, although you retire me or not from your abode, but your image 'll remain with a suppressed modality and impression for ever. May I beg my

Master to free me of my awe and bless me a free flow stream of 'bhakti' for time boundless?"

The cry of bleeding mother-heart, melts the brittle heart of the mighty 'Yamraja'. Finally the cry of the mother compelled the entire heaven and the Almighty. Lord Vishnu appeared to the 'yam Lok' and advised Yam raja to send back Renuka once again in the same physical attire and age to the same identity which she had to the same person who is the son in the earth , of her.

Maharaja Yam drove into the ocean of huge concern, how a soul of dead woman be send down? Lord vishnu, the 'palan har'(protector of the universe) carries the string of every concerns and pull and loose in appropriate time. Lord instructed Yam raja , another pious soul of same aged woman, who was just the mirror image of Renuka has appeared to the yamlok and her physical attire is some where hidden in the deep jungle of the cliffs of Darjeeling.

Renuka's soul brims more in devotion and bliss. She fell into the feet of lord Vishnu. Lord felt pleased with her love and devotion towards Him on earth and now, He takes her into His arms; He blessed her for a new and prosperous journey in the mortal world and instructed her to be more committed and dedicated towards her Guru, who is Himself in mortal figure and role. In this second course of life Renuka would be marked with profound activities of devotion towards her 'isht dev', the Lord and guru on earth, who is none but Almighty Lord Vishnu, along with her family. Lord said her,"My child this is your continuous silent chanting of 'naam', holy name of her 'isht dev' even in the death bed, which stirred me to come to you; my child you will be blessed with another attire of gleeful deed and all in your world would accept you like earlier. Remember ' naam' and 'isht' way of life, bring more and influence more people in the earth for me. This life would be an exemplary for the eras to come on Earth".

Similarly, shina too got pampered from the Lord and loved her just like a sweet child. She is blessed the eternal life in heaven.

Chapter-25

Lord smiled at Shina, "Shina my child you have suffered a lot through out your life , but you never forgot me nor your godly qualities stepped down in your character. All these were due to your pre birth karmic consequences that you suffered. Now you are free of all karmic shackles. You are free from all the series of life and death. My child here you are having one more surprise, your sashi is waiting long for you, go and enjoy your love here in this new abode, new garden, the eternal garden..." Shina bows down into the feet of lord. She expressed, her mortal attire is fallen unknown and her soul has a pinch of pain for letting her murderer untouched by any evidence. Then, the Lord exclaimed, " every thing is stringed by me, as they had sown so shall they reap. You need not to worry, they 'll be punished, now you say, my child how do you want to treat them, the murderer of your mortal being?" hearing lord, Shina said, " Let all people in my village know my brothers and kartar, how they had destroyed my love, my peace and my life in earth". " so my child what would you want next from your part ?" said lord Vishnu smilingly. For a while Shina paused and then expressed, " I want all the three miscreants to be punished by the law of the land. I want to reveal the probe of evidence which they had concealed for ever". Lord blessed her soul as she desired. Shina with the power of lord puffed up to accomplish her revenge. Lord blessed both the souls and instructs, Yamraja to guide and help fully to Renuka to come down on earth. With these words lord mingled into the ether.

Shina's soul at the dark end of night moved into her village from a public telephone booth rang the local police station and talked to the inspector in charge, Mr. Bhagat Singh sodhi. She told the entire story of her abduction from Punjab to Darjeeling and poisoning her and finally strangling her to death. Besides she asserted the exact time of train, the cab number to carry her to Darjeeling from shiliguri; and the 'dupatta' which was thrown aside in the jungle. The police man asked who she was talking all these unearthly story at the dead end of the night. She put down the phone. The cop thought it to be a fun played for making him fool. No action was stepped by the police. Next night again at the same hour of darkness Shina gave a ring to the police station. She repeated the same story. But getting no response. The next night she appeared to the police station. The gust of wind in the chilly night wide opened the door of the police station, looking at the appearance of Shina , sodhi sank back into his chair. Shina repeated the story for the third time to him and the cop remained wide eye opened just listened her with awful look. He couldn't speak a single word. Shina just alarmingly said to him , " if you take an action it's good for you". The unearthly body disappeared silently.

The cop from the next morning stepped serious foot to dig out all the probe Shina had mentioned. He only could not find the body of Shina, the reason was beyond his investigation. With all probe uncarthed, he arrested the three miscreants and the truth of Shina's disappearance unveiled in front of the villagers. All cried and and remained heavy hearted for Shina, the innocent and pure lady who lived only for others. All were assured with the evidence Shina was no more in this planet.

Sodhi shrank again when a phone rang up at the same hour of midnight. There was the voice of the same woman- Shina. She thanked the inspector and clarified all about her death. Sodhi could not sleep for a couple of days after that phonic conversation. His tranquiled mind got pacified only after arranging a 'satsang kirtan' at the police station with the help of the villagers. That was a hilarious all around.

Chapter-26

In the meanwhile, according to lord of the Lords instructions, the soul of urging mother, Renuka was lit into the physical attire of Shina; the body that was hidden from the world in the deep cliffs of Darjeeling.

Yamraja led Renuka to the cliffs of Darjeeling and instructed Renuka "Now do as I say". Renuka very astonishingly glared at the laid body of her look and touched the new body. "Maharaj its just me" exclaimed Renuka. " now enter into it", said Yamraja. "but how Maharaj"? Very softly Renuka asked. " you sleep on the body as if the body is yours." This is Shina's body who is identical to you. Yamraja informed her, "There will be some great drama and clash of identity when you'll be reunited with your own family in the body of Shina, so be prepared for any situation, and follow my all instructions. "Maharaj, how can I regain my status of previous being, what reason or prove I may present to the mortal people that I am Renuka. All know that Renuka is no more, she is cremated". Maharaja simply smiled and answered her, " Never be over anxious about your future, when Master of the universe has blessed you for a new birth in old identity then it would be definitely wended. No force ,no star, none can bar that happening. Everything is on His will He can make day into night and vice-versa, if He wishes He can lit a vanished soul in the world once again. All science is guided by him. All logics and science is beneath His power. All is His play. Your re-birth would be an instance for the " Kali yuga". Master of masters has scripted something new to the man world to show His presence, boldly. Time demands to glimpse the light of the God through you now. This play is beyond normal man's concern."

Renuka enters into the lifeless body of Shina. She bowed to the Yamraja and expressed her gratitude, " I am really very lucky enough to play the direct role in the play of the only playwright of the universe". " You'll be taken to Haridwar, there you would serve our Lord in the big temple by the river Ganga, after a period of your serve to the Master of this universe, you would be led to your world of family where you have left your loving son and daughter-in-law, and other admirers besides a new member to your family whom you had expected since very long". Said Yamraja. "A new member?" exclaimed Renuka . " yes that's surprise awaits for you, now just keep pumping that surprise in your heart to have but with sheer patience, and follow me up to Haridwar and keep my words what you are to do there now".

Renuka took a pause, "A new member,…..who can it be besides my grand children from Ragini? Does she has a new born again…? No I don't think so. Maharaj has said new member into my home, whom I have been awaited for long…" smile of elation fulfilled her heart and face.

"Then for God I'm sure , this might be the lamp of our clan; Ritutaj's child. How impatiently I've been waited and dried up my eyes and baked my heart to have a glimpse and hear the sound of my own grand child from my son." She sobbed and fervent enough to meet her monsoon for baked heart and spring for her eyes.

In the next moment she became very serene and surrendered all to the wish of Lord and the Maharaj.

Chapter-27

Again 'Yamraja' asserted Renuka "When time will come, I would reach to you". Renuka is led to the big Sri Krishna mandir and there taking holy bath of re-birth in the Ganga at night she fell before the idol of the Lord; who was standing . She could absorb the blessings of the Lord in to her mind and body from the enlightened idol. In her eyes there was no pain or prick of death. Her physical attire was totally toned up and her heart became more austere than earlier. While bowing down before the Lord she lost her nerves and sense. She forgot all the in between happenings at her absent days. Only one thing was set in her mind that she had come to Darjeeling with her family there she lost the way and abducted. From her abduction she was rescued by the big brother, who was the god of death, and led her way to the Haridwar. The big brother is very robust and powerful, he is very just and follow the Masters of this universe very strictly, very religiously. She had a firm belief that only the big brother will bring back her into the family world when she would meet definitely when right time approaches. Her brother would come and lead her to her mortal abode.

 When she opened her eyes she found the pandits and the pujari of the temple sprinkling holy water in her face.

Renuka wake up and first glance fell upon the big brother standing beside the idol of the Lord Krishna. She wake up as if after a long deep sleep. She remembered only the words of the big brother. The pujari of the temple asked her where about and who she was? She could say nothing and cried very poorly, " I cannot recollect any thing in my mind, please help me and provide me a shelter at the feet of the Lord so that I can serve Him day and night. I have no idea how I am here". Pujariji and other pandits felt for the poor Renuka and said, "sister this is the home of our Lord of whole universe all unsheltered are sheltered in His benevolence, you are here with His gracious wish". So Renuka got a carnal welcome in the home of the Lord.

The Yam raja vanished after blessing Renuka straight her eyes.

Renuk started her duty with full devotion , she plucked and collected flowers, made garlands, washed the utensils of 'bhog' of Lord, washed clothes of Lord , helped in preparing 'bhog' at the kitchen. She sang prayer and 'bhajans' along with other devotees .She listened to the pain and suffering of other people who ever came to the temple and talked to Renuka. All were pleased with Renuka and felt blessed to share with her. Whenever she was asked about her family and life, she only smiled, a smile of bliss and said, " Only Lord is my family and all devotees come here are my kin. He has sent me in the earth , He plays several 'Leelas'(play) with us and at His Will I am here."

The eyes of Renuka brimmed with full devotion and smile. She never recalled of her son nor her daughter and others of past life. But she knew what was happening to her was all His blessed wish and she would be placed in right time in right place.

Chapter-28

After spending a life of pilgrimage for around couple of years in Haridwar, it's now time for Sri Hari Vishnu to place Renuka in her early life. Thus appeared the Big brother , Yamraja in his robust stature with big mustachio and in black dhoti and black shawl; as if a 'tapaswi' of truth and follower of the Lord. Straight, He entered the temple of Haridwar, where He had left Renuka years ago and met the pujari and all pandits, He talked to them about Renuka's where about , he addressed himself to be Renuka's big brother and after quenching liters of sweat and toil from northeast to Darjeeling, finally got her trace in Haridwar. All were convinced to accept him. The main 'purohit' of the temple wanted to get clear more about the relationship of the stranger and Renuka. He called out Renuka , " sister do you know this man? He is looking for a lady like you". " oh, my big brother…" with a confident smile at her face. The purohit understood the depth of their relationship and decided to send Renuka along with him to her family, she had forgotten partially. But the local devotees and staunch lover of Renuka were disheartened, they didn't want to release Renuka from their propinquity so easily. All started crying and impelled her to remain their kin always. Big brother prayed all, " Don't you all want to reunite a son with her mother, she was such a misfortune soul who even doesn't know whom she had been detached from so far and wandering like a destitute, being the big brother, I am in sheer distress and worried about my sister, and in great responsibility to reintegrate ". He now with bold voice wanted to take all's leave along with Renuka.

After paying all her gratitude to the 'mandir wasis'(temple community) and bowing down before Lord she started with her big brother.

Chapter-29

Almost after four years of her bereavement from her son and others Renuka re-appeared one fine morning along with her big brother. This was a thud to all the present members at the new house of rituraj. The neighbors were all shocked with awe . One of the lady shrieked in fear, " ….. ghost of Renuka" and she lost her nerves. All were mostly in a state of quandary.

By this four years time, Rituraj had built a dream house rather a bungalow of his father's vision and the house which his beloved mother had had thought all the time to have. A house which would have a big mandir for her Gurudev to worship with all peace and devotion. The temple for God would be facilitated with good water supply, big 'singhashana', well lighted and ventilated, all sorts of comfort to her God with dresses and clothes. The bungalow of Rituraj was highlighted with that dream mandir(temple). The spacious house was having a good ground for gardening, playing and maintaining a well kitchen garden. By this time Rituraj had bought a car and was established well in his society

He became a renowned personality of the town. Everybody knew him to be religious, honest and a charitable person. In fact a person of humanity.

Rituraj, the only fellow who was producing a contented smile with silent thankful pray to his Lord. He was having strong belief that some day her mother would definitely come back to him, she cannot leave him such. He knew firmly the continue pray of a son might be heard by the Master of the life and death whether early or later. In fact Rituraj had sobbed uncounted days and nights alone, praying like a mad to his Lord and had a firm light of belief, his mother would reunite him very soon.

He knew it very well his Lord never deaf his pray . His remaining duty for his mother ought to be served by him and he would not be kept empty handed of his prayer.

It was pouring outside glittering with sunshine.

Rituraj stood up like lightning and hug her wide with huge cry and tears in his eyes, "maa…."; the time of reunion a son with his mother appeared like a huge gallon of water from a tide, dam unblocked forcibly. He cried a loud and uttered all his grief buried for last few years of dissection from his piece of heart. " maa , I'm an extinguished lamp for past few years, I'm just a pit of dumb, a closed book , a dead body just carrying life in disguise. There I feel very less air to inhale fresh. Maa, you knew well you are only my life air, you are only my light of life; without air and light how your son can lead a life of zeal? Your love lap is my pillow, without it how can I sleep? Maa I am very thirsty... I am very thirsty. Without you in my life I'm a loser. Now I regain my victory, my light, my air. I am in life again……". Rituraj hugged his mother tightly and both cried high as if to make almighty sobbed. Rain droplets outside metaphorically signed that moment. The sunshine accompanied with rain described the whole circumstances of the remarkable day.

All were thunder stricken with awe. Renuka had gain a lot of teachings in these years of life. She earned bliss, peace and a smile in face all time. She could learn all is His wish, our existence, our whereabouts, our move in life is all stringed by Lord. So nothing to tense about if you are to think and stir your mind and heart it should be for Him and nothing in this mortal world. We are sent in this mortal world and relation just to perform temporary duties with complete remembrance of Lord and doing all for soul purpose of human life, that is 'serve your God'.

The big brother took the sit in an arm chair offered by Rituraj greeting him whole heartedly. Rituraj fell at His feet and asked Him about the journey up to his house. Big brother smiled at him. All were murmuring and curious to know how this could be happened; a dead person cannot come back, who this fellow is in black attire. One among the crowd asked all the curiosity of the mass mind to the big fellow.

Now Yamraja, starts His thunderous tone and says very firm, " she is my sister, and very loving , I come to know all about her for last three years and now I give her to her son. I found her swerving in the roads of Darjeeling, she was so scared that she could not speak anything about her. She seemed to be tantalized and extremely effected psychologically. I decided then to keep her in a safe place where her mental stability may regain and she may come to her normalcy. Thus I bring her along with me to Haridwar to my known big temple of Sri Krishna. She was given shelter by the mandir committee. I looked after her beside our Lord the savior of our life. It is His wish, that blessed her to serve Him there and serve all His devotees come there. She won the love, respect and compassion from every body in Haridwar; for last three years she was the pull of all devotees and mankind . She served all with her pious heart.

Each and every body armed as if salvation with her touch and conversation with her was soothing and blissful. But nobody knew rather tried to know her personal life. She is such a poor woman who had forgotten every deed and action of her past life when came to her sense after repose for few days after leaving Darjeeling to Haridwar. But as I found her first, I felt for her like a big brother, who needs a support. A new support for a new journey."

From the crowd, one old lady asked the old man, " but Renuka is dead since years around, how can she come from Haridwar?" " This is quite dramatic and might be some fraud".

Renuka cried bitterly, " yes I was dead for last few years, I am without my son and my family. You all know very well, we had been to Darjeeling, we were enjoying there natural beauty and jocund environment; but one day some unknown fellows for unknown reason abducted me and I don't know, why my son had left me without a search, whether he and my daughter in law felt disturbed of my company in their life , I don't know? From Darjeeling I had been taken to the direction of north India as I heard and they were planning to finish me. When I asked them, why they are killing an innocent old lady who even don't know any thing of their activities? They got puzzled and asked my name and where about. Hearing Bengali and mixed Hindi in which there was no touch of Punjabi, they paused their planning in fact murderous plan and left me free after a long discussion among themselves. But I was abandoned in the unknown valley of siliguri. Anyhow I could earn the sympathy of a 'pahaari' gentleman going towards Darjeeling on his goods car. He led me up to Darjeeling. I thought I may reach to my son but I couldn't find the place and hotel they had boarded. No local dared to help me much. And I wandered all the streets and roads of the hilly area like a mad, un-food and wretched health condition. I almost became a lunatic as every body started thinking of me. Even I lost my faith and believe from life. But it might be my spontaneous Guru mantra that had met me with my big brother who can be none but God himself. Next, you all heard".

"But we've seen you with your son and family, we have talked with you; we have seen you suffering for long one year and we have seen your son performing all post mortal rituals for your soul. Who was then she?" Said one of the neighbors.

I know nothing, what are you all saying, I don't remember anything except Haridwar, my Lord, serving mankind, and pious feet of Lord Krishna." Said Renuka.

All were remained open mouth. Only Rituraj sobbed at the feet of his mother and thankfully bowed before the messenger of God. There was a huge Repercussion and murmuring all around. Some advised Rituraj "she can't be your mother perhaps she is a ghost…" . Some assumed her to be evil and may cause harm to his family. From the flow of such exegesis, few philosophical dialogs aired up. " this is punarjanm of Renuka….." "….. the magic boon of God which is very rare to notice in this Kali yuga" etc etc. Most of the crowd demanded Renuka to be out and away. An upheaval arouse in the crowd. This was the presumed clash to be happened. Big brother took the chaos very calmly, "if anybody is having any doubt, you can cross check her with all evidences or question related to her past life. You might have various instances or occasions along with Renuka, which others might not know"! Many arrows of queries thrown towards Renuka. She propitiated all very dearly.

Chapter-30

Rituraj now became very restless and with whole heart tried to serve his mother's big brother. " Mama what will you like to have?" " nothing my son, I'll take your leave now, I am very much enamored with your attachment for your mother. I suppose you have got the bird in bush, I hope this time you would not miss the Vantage. Remember son this juncture comes rarest in an interval of long epoch. Lord has chosen the media that is you, His flag of spiritualism in the mundane life for the fair stretching of humanism, letting the light of love, faith, and promoting divine relation in this earth, you will be the polestar of the era. You and your family are really the providential. Remember Him do and go for His purpose." He paused for a while, and sighed, " Remember, in this caducous life, mother is the only biggest asset than anything, never bargain her with any thing". Rituraj's mind could access half of his speech clearly, mostly impalpable. He washed the feet of the pious old man and wiped them off with a white new dhoti. Beside him his wife and Renuka along with the new member of their family bow down into his feet, all they prayed His blessings for their normal life of love and spirituality. Rituraj sobbed and tear rolled down from his eyes. His tear expressed many thing of faith and his quest of heart to his Lord was quenched for ever.

" Mama shower your blessings upon our family to remain United for ever and go ahead only for our loving Lord. I was bereft of my maa, my life had gone desert for past few years. I want to serve my Lord along with my maa and wife and the new member, my son. I want the boon of evergreen in heart to a son. I know you are none other than God messenger to respond this poor sobbing heart of a son. My Lord, bless this poor son so that the kingdom of son's heart may never get barren of mother's love, without maa life's any activity or achievement is valueless, lifeless, when living God is with me, my presence is meaningful else my right to live is useless. Don't let me to be a failure, in heart of my Lord and mother Earth".

The big stature smiled at him and hold him in his heart and said, " look Rituraj, it Is your love that brings your mother back to you. I'm very glad in fact God is very glad to bless you your mother back after such a long gap. Now you remember one thing along with your mother , wife and child serve only your Lord, do all possibilities to Him to please Him. I bless you my child…… and Renuka go get your monsoon of heart and spring of dried eyes fast". He smiled contentedly seeing Renuka happy like never before.

Concluding His speech He took leave of all very hast. He didn't disclose his identity . Just one thing he revealed from his conversation that he is an ardent follower and servant of Lord Vishnu .

www.ingramcontent.com/pod-product-compliance
Lightning Source LLC
LaVergne TN
LVHW091551170726
843492LV00007B/2134